P9-DNW-091

GOES TO THE DENTIST

Adapted from the Curious George film series
edited by Margret Rey and Alan J. Shalleck

1 9 8 9
Houghton Mifflin Company, Boston

Library of Congress Cataloging-in-Publication Data

Curious George goes to the dentist/edited by Margret Rey and Alan J.
Shalleck.
p. cm.
"Adapted from the Curious George film series."
Summary: Curious George accompanies his friend to the dentist's
office and helps alleviate a girl's fear of the chair.
ISBN 0-395-51941-1
[1. Monkeys–Fiction. 2. Dental care–Fiction.] I. Rey,
Margret. II. Shalleck, Alan J. III. Curious George goes to the
dentist (Motion picture)
PZ7.C92183 1989 89-32364
[E]–dc20 CIP
AC

Printed in the United States of America

Y 10 9 8 7 6 5 4 3 2 1

“Ouch!” said George’s friend.
“I’ve got a bad toothache.
I must go and see the dentist.”

When they arrived at the dentist's office, a nurse said,
"Dr. Huggins will take you right away, sir."

"George, you wait out here
in the waiting room," said the man.

George sat down beside a little girl and her mother.
The little girl looked unhappy.

“I don’t want to go in there,” the little girl said.
“Dr. Huggins won’t hurt you,” said her mother.
“But those machines make scary noises,” the little girl said.

A nurse came in and said, “We’re all ready, Mrs. Campbell.
Would Melissa like to go in first?”

Melissa started to cry.
"There's nothing to worry about, Melissa," said Mrs. Campbell.
"I'll go first, okay?"

Mrs. Campbell left with the nurse.

George picked up a book and started to read.
He and Melissa waited.

After a while, George got restless.

He got up and looked around.
The door to the examining room was open.

George sneaked by the nurse at the desk and went in.

In the examining room, a nurse was putting cotton into Mrs. Campbell's mouth.

Mrs. Campbell was sitting in a strange-looking chair.
It had all sorts of levers and knobs and pedals.

How did that chair work? George was curious.

The nurse was gone, so he went over and
pulled one of the levers.

The chair started to rise.

He stepped on a pedal…

...and the chair turned around.

George gave Mrs. Campbell quite a ride.
But Mrs. Campbell didn't want a ride!

By this time, Melissa had come to the door
of the examining room to see what was going on. She was smiling.

Just then, the nurse came running back.
"You get away from that chair, George," she scolded.

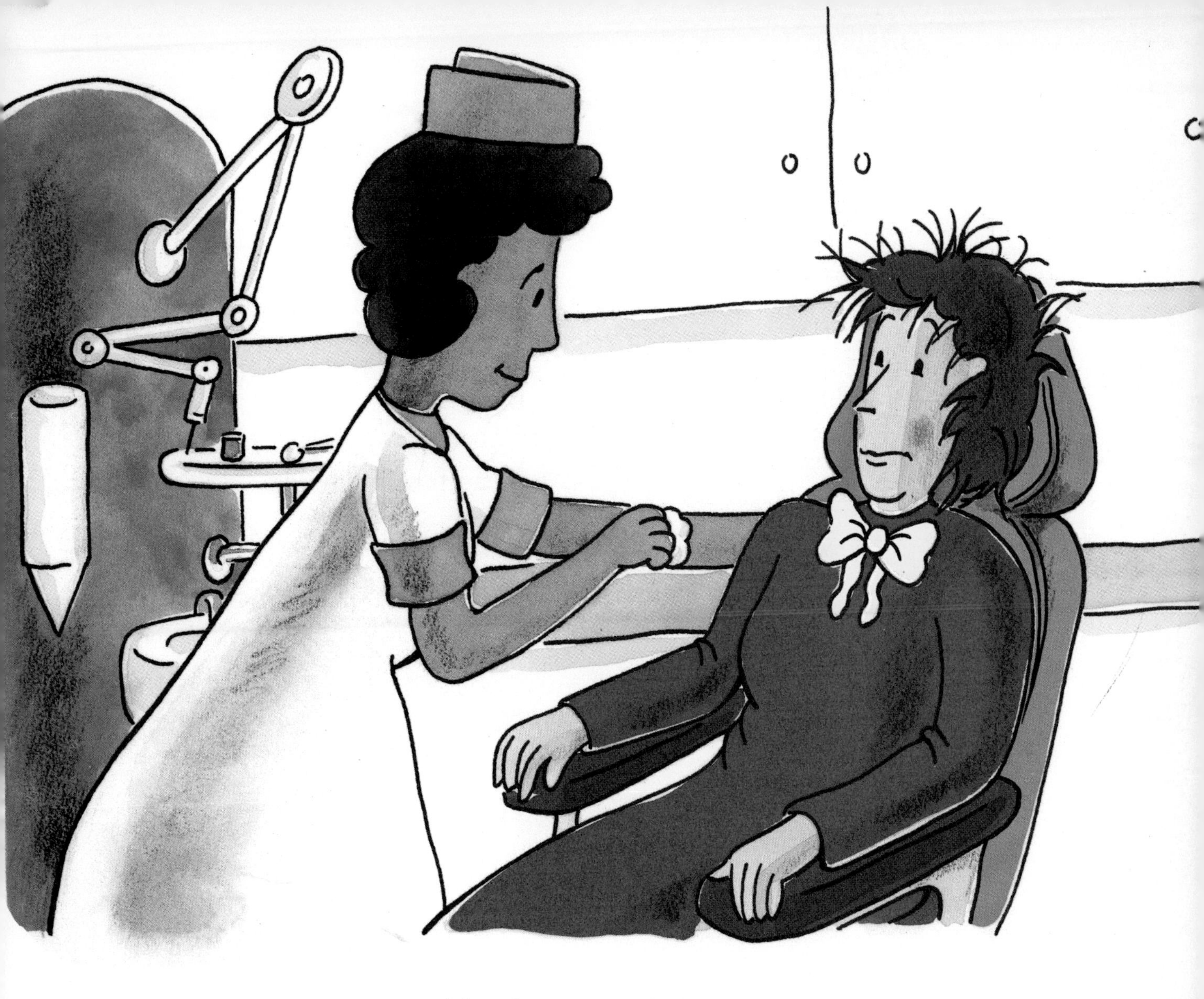

Quickly, she stopped the chair and
took the cotton out of Mrs. Campbell's mouth.

Mrs. Campbell was very angry. “That monkey was bothering me!” she shouted.

“I’ll go and get Dr. Huggins right away!” said the nurse.

"What's going on here?" asked the doctor.
George was scared and hid behind the chair.
"It's that little monkey down there," said the nurse.

Suddenly, Melissa laughed. "I think George is funny," she said.
"When can I get into that chair?
I want a ride, too."

Dr. Huggins smiled.

Mrs. Campbell smiled, too.

"George," she said, "I didn't like the ride you gave me,
but you stopped Melissa from
being afraid of the dentist. Thank you!"